1

This Walker book belongs to:

REX
AND
PRINCESS VICTORIA

WALKER BOOKS
AND SUBSIDIARIES
LONDON · BOSTON · SYDNEY · AUCKLAND

Historic
Royal Palaces

One sunny afternoon, after the last visitors had left the Tower of London, Rex trotted to his favourite litter bin to find a snack.

He burrowed down,
past banana skins and greasy chips
– and suddenly he felt himself
falling back in time.

He tumbled and turned
and twisted around,

and hit the ground with a

THUD !

Rex scrambled to his feet. He wasn't at the Tower of London any more. He was outside a big redbrick house – a *really* big redbrick house. I wonder who lives here? he thought. And I wonder if they have any treats?

Rex was trotting around the garden when his nose started twitching with the unmistakable smell of another dog. A happy-looking spaniel was bouncing towards him.

"Hello! A visitor!" panted the spaniel. "We never have
   visitors at Kensington Palace! What's your name?"
"Rex," said Rex.
"I'm Dash," said the spaniel. "Are you here
   to see her Royal Highness?"
"Her Royal Highness? Who's that?" asked Rex.
"Princess Victoria, of course," said Dash.
"Maybe. Will she give me some dog biscuits?"
"What are dog biscuits? She gives me cake
   when no one's looking…"
   Rex liked the sound of that.
"Then yes, I *am* here to
   see her," he said.

Rex had expected the palace to be grand inside, but Dash led him
up a dark, scruffy staircase. They stopped outside an open door.
"This is the princess's room," whispered Dash.
A girl was sitting at a desk, looking very tired and very bored,
as a grey-haired man fired questions at her.

"Poor Princess Victoria," said Dash. "She has lessons with Mr Davys every single day apart from Sunday."
"I thought princesses could do what they liked," said Rex.
"Not at all! She isn't even allowed her own bedroom," said Dash. "She has to share with her mother!"

After a while, Mr Davys gave a little nod.
"That will be all for today," he said.
The dogs saw their chance, and as he left, they slipped inside.

When Princess Victoria saw the dogs, she clapped her hands. "Dash! And who's this?" she said, scratching Rex behind the ears. "Would you like to come for a walk?"

But a stern voice behind them said, "I'm not sure your mother would approve. She doesn't like you mixing with strangers. Not even strange dogs."

Rex turned to see a neat-looking woman standing in the doorway.

"That's Lehzen," said Dash. "She's Princess Victoria's governess."

"Please, Lehzen—" started Victoria. But Lehzen ignored her.

"I'm going to fetch my coat. While you're waiting for me,
  send that scruffy dog back into the streets."
  Victoria frowned as Lehzen left the room.

"I wish I were a dog. I'd go wherever I liked."
  She looked at the dogs and smiled suddenly.

"You've given me an idea. If I wanted to run
  away, you'd help me, wouldn't you?"
  The dogs wagged their tails.

"Let's go now, before
  Lehzen comes back!"
  said the princess,
  snatching up
  her bonnet.

They tiptoed down the staircase and ran to the stables, where a pony and trap stood waiting.

"Bark if you see anyone coming!" said Victoria, as they all jumped in. She patted the pony and cried, "Run like the wind, Rosie!"

As Rosie began to gallop out of the palace gates, Rex barked
– someone was at the window. Victoria gasped. "It's Lehzen!"
"Come back this instant!" cried Lehzen.
But the princess shook her head. "We'll be back by bedtime!
Please don't tell Mamma!"

They cantered through the streets of London
until they reached a smart, grassy square.
Victoria tied Rosie up and grinned at the dogs.
"Now," she said. "Let's have some fun…"

They played hoop
along Pall Mall,

and rowed a boat in
Hyde Park,

and ate the most delicious
cake in the whole city.

Rex had never had such a wonderful afternoon.
And then, as the sun went down, they walked through
Piccadilly Circus and queued for tickets at the theatre.
"Marie Taglioni is performing tonight," breathed Princess
Victoria. "She's the most wonderful dancer in the world!"

Victoria watched, enchanted, as Mademoiselle Taglioni twirled across the stage. Rex and Dash were more interested in the scraps of food on the floor.

When the ballet was over, everyone stood and cried, "Brava!" "Encore!" And then Mademoiselle Taglioni curtseyed to the royal box…

Everyone turned to look. A woman with a large
feather in her hat was smiling at the crowds.
"That's the Duchess of Kent!" hissed Dash.
"She's Princess Victoria's mother!"
Victoria gasped and hid her face behind her playbill.
"Quick – I have to get home before she does!"

"Hurry! This way!"
barked Rex.
They ran into the
street – just as
the duchess
swept past.

"We must get back to the palace before her!" whispered Victoria,
as the duchess got into the royal carriage. "What can we do?"
A nearby crossing sweeper heard Victoria's cry.
"Can I help you, Miss?"
he said, bowing low.
"Yes!" said Victoria.
"Stop that carriage!"
The boy ran out in
front of the royal
carriage and waved
his arms.

"This road's closed!" he cried. "You've got to go
that way…" He pointed down a tiny alleyway.
The driver grumbled and nodded as the carriage trundled
off in the wrong direction. The boy winked at Victoria.
"Thank you!" she said as she clambered
into her trap. "Giddy up, Rosie! Let's go!"

Back at the palace, Victoria tossed her things
onto her dressing table and jumped into bed.
"Go, before Mamma catches you!" she
whispered to Rex.
But there were footsteps on the stairs…

"In here!" said Dash, and Rex followed him into a cupboard.
"We'll have to hide in here till the duchess falls asleep…"
 But suddenly Princess Victoria sat upright in bed and hissed,
"My playbill from the theatre – I left it on the dressing table!
 Mamma will see it. She'll know where I've been!"

Rex didn't hesitate. He jumped out of the cupboard
and snatched the playbill from the dressing table – just
as Victoria's mother walked through the door.
"Help! A dog! A dirty, scruffy dog!" she screamed.
"What's that you've got in your mouth?"
Before she could grab the playbill, Rex ran out of the room.
Victoria and the duchess chased after him.

"Stop! Thief!" cried the duchess.
Rex raced out onto the grass,
so fast he felt his legs might fly off.
But the duchess was catching up…
Just then, he smelt something
stinky, something juicy,
something extremely delicious.

His litter bin!

As he dived in, he heard
Princess Victoria whisper.
"Thank you!" she said.
"You're welcome!"
barked Rex.
And then he fell
into blackness.

Rex landed with a THUD on Tower Green.

"Eating rubbish again?" called a Yeoman Warder.

"Where did you get this from?"

If only you knew, thought Rex. But at least

he was back in time for dinner.

Also available from Walker Books:

"A really good read"
— *Made for Mums*

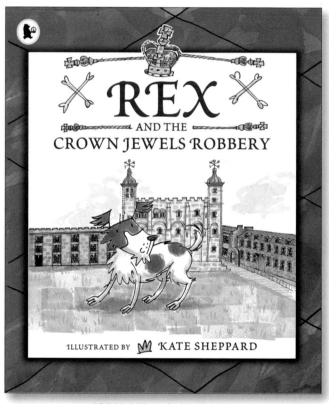

ISBN 978-1-4063-6069-1

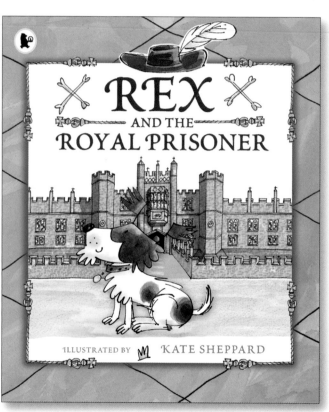

ISBN 978-1-4063-6606-8

Available from all good booksellers

www.walker.co.uk

This book is inspired by Queen Victoria's childhood at
Kensington Palace, where she was born in 1819. She really did have
lessons every day apart from Sunday and had to share a bedroom
with her mother until she became queen in 1837!
To find out more please visit:

www.hrp.org.uk

First published 2017 by Walker Books Ltd, 87 Vauxhall Walk, London SE11 5HJ
in association with Historic Royal Palaces, Hampton Court Palace, Surrey KT8 9AU

10 9 8 7 6 5 4 3 2 1

© 2017 Historic Royal Palaces and Walker Books Ltd

This book has been typeset in Garamond

Printed in China

British Library Cataloguing in Publication Data: a catalogue record for this book is available from the British Library

ISBN 978-1-4063-7299-1

www.walker.co.uk

Bumps in the Night

ALLAN AHLBERG • ANDRÉ AMSTUTZ

PUFFIN

In the dark dark cellar
of a dark dark house,
a little skeleton is reading a comic.
In the dark dark street
of a dark dark town,
a big skeleton is walking the dog.

Then the big one hurries home,
and the little one hurries out,
and – "Help!" –
they go bump in the night.

In the dark dark classroom
of a dark dark Night School,
a little skeleton is painting a picture.
In the dark dark workshop
of the same Night School,
a big skeleton is making a chair.

Then the little one takes his picture
to show the big one,
and the big one takes his chair
to show the little one,
and – "Wow!" –
they go bump in the night again.

"Send for Doctor Bones!"

The little skeleton and the big skeleton
walk *carefully* to the park.
They swing on the swings,
throw a stick for the dog
and play football.

"The leg bone's connected to the foot bone,"
the little one sings.
"The foot bone's connected to the ball."

"The head bone's connected
to the – (CLONK!) – head bone,"
cries the big one.

"Send for Doctor Bones!"

The little skeleton and
the big skeleton sit
– but not too close together –
in the dark dark cellar.
"This is a dark dark cellar,"
says the little one. "Let's paint it."
"Good idea!" the big one says.

The big skeleton
and the little skeleton
paint the cellar
and, now and then, the dog.

They paint the cellar
red and green and blue,
and lots more colours.

But . . .
"It's still dark,"
the little skeleton says.
"Let's paint it white."
So, they paint it white . . .

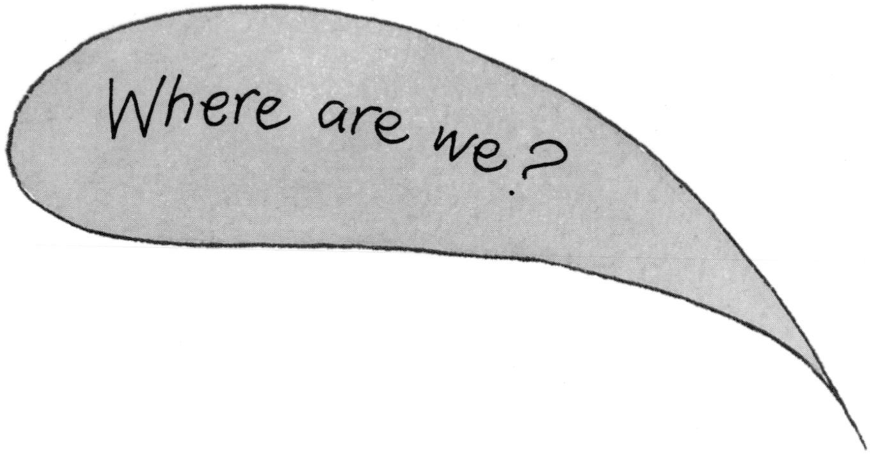
Where are we?

and disappear!
And – you guessed it –
go bump in the night.

"Send for Doctor Bones!"

After that . . .
they go bump in the night playing tennis
and bump in the night playing golf.

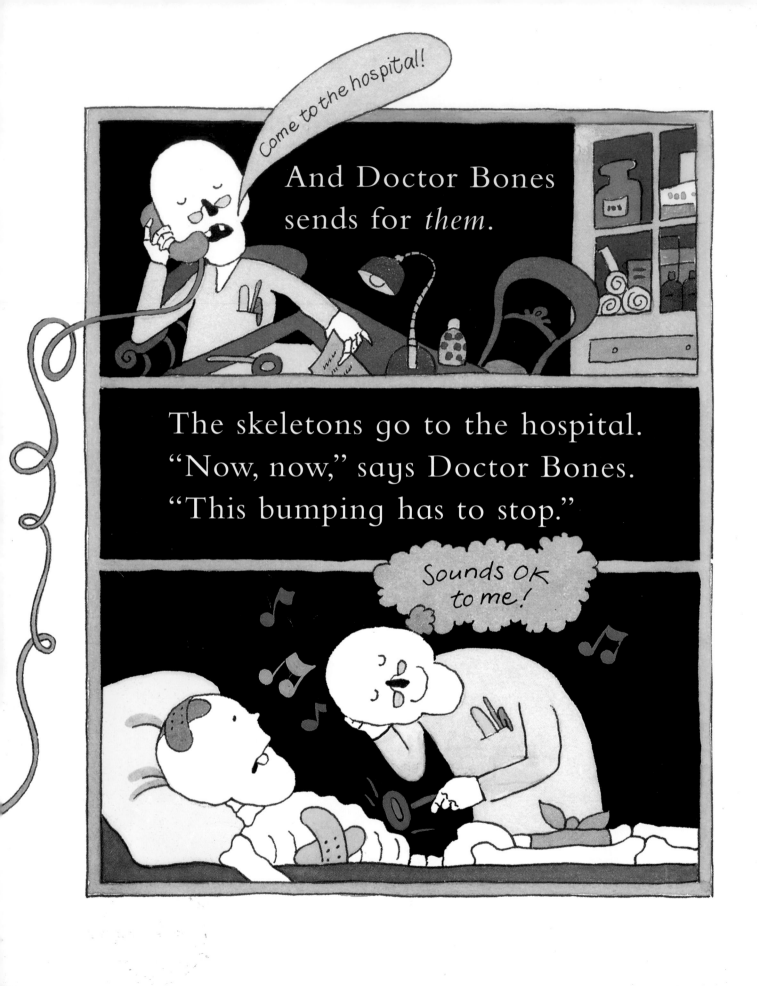

In the dark dark cellar
(they painted it black again)
of a dark dark house,
a little skeleton is fast asleep.
"Zzz!"
In the same cellar of the same house,
a big skeleton is fast asleep too.
"Zzz!"

There they are . . .
tucked up snug and safe at last
from bumps in the night.

Well, nearly.

The End

PUFFIN BOOKS

Published by the Penguin Group
Penguin Books Ltd, 80 Strand, London WC2R 0RL, England
Penguin Group (USA), Inc., 375 Hudson Street, New York, New York 10014, USA
Penguin Books Australia Ltd, 250 Camberwell Road, Camberwell, Victoria 3124, Australia
Penguin Books Canada Ltd, 10 Alcorn Avenue, Toronto, Ontario, Canada M4V 3B2
Penguin Books India (P) Ltd, 11 Community Centre, Panchsheel Park, New Delhi – 110 017, India
Penguin Group (NZ), cnr Airborne and Rosedale Roads, Albany, Auckland 1310, New Zealand
Penguin Books (South Africa) (Pty) Ltd, 24 Sturdee Avenue, Rosebank 2196, South Africa

Penguin Books Ltd, Registered Offices: 80 Strand, London WC2R 0RL, England

www.penguin.com

First published by William Heinemann Ltd 1993
First published in Puffin Books 2005
1 3 5 7 9 10 8 6 4 2

British Library Cataloguing in Publication Data
A CIP catalogue record for this book is available from the British Library

ISBN 0-140-56684-8